Sea Shadows

Sharing the Joys and Challenges through Poetry and Prose

Ron Autrey

For permission requests, email the publisher at the address below.

E.P. House
hello@ephouse.co

This is a creative work, the views and experiences expressed are those of the author.

First edition – December 2025
Hardcover ISBN: 979-8-9881881-6-2

PRINTED IN THE UNITED STATES OF AMERICA ON ACID-FREE PAPER

www.ephouse.co
Cover designed by Kerry Jesberger

To my wife Hilah, who brings
beauty and excitement
to our daily existence, I am here to share
my life through writing because of her
love and support

Contents

Introduction

Where the Ocean Meets the Sky

Where the ocean meets the sky
There is a marriage of the wind with waves.
Every day brings new adventure.

Some days are more calm than others,
Others more rough than calm.

Through every storm, the waves and wind
Crest and fall.
The calm returns,
The sky turns blue,
And another day passes
Quietly by . . .

Why Poetry?

Some people see beautiful images and paintings, hear music, or take photographs. I see beautiful scenes and people, and words come to mind. I like to soften the prose and add a hint of syntax, making the words a probe into your senses so they become your words, your thoughts.

PART I:
Patriotism

American Battle Drums

Hear the American battle drums
In "My Country, 'Tis of Thee."
Our world is lost in dark and doubt,
We must implore, don't take your knee …
Rise up, stand tall, and clearly shout!
"America the Beautiful" is our song to sing.
To slash with words the twisted thoughts,
Pound the drums 'til freedom rings!

Hopes for Peace

Artists write: “Let’s come together,”
But not how hard it would be
To win the hearts and ease the minds
Of those who will not see.

Forced farther apart,
Each challenging day,
Our troubled hearts so hollow.
We hope and we pray
For peace in our thoughts
And a fair path to follow.

The day will come, and all will learn
That peace is not a gift.
It is a reward worth working for,
A prize we all must earn.

For me, I’ll pray
That peace will come to the beauty that surrounds us.
The singing birds and skies so blue
Say that God is still among us.

I hope before the end of days
Our dream will be fulfilled.
His path will mend our wicked ways

And God will have his will.

Pray then, our hearts
Once broken,
Will forever now be healed.

A Soldier's Lament

Lest ye think my heart hardened as the lead of musket balls,
I'll lend ye my early morning thoughts.
They struck me clean from my bed
With a notion that words and not swords
Be my weapon of choice this day.

Lend me your ear, I'll tell ye straight.
The blood and death will not save us.
We the people, with clear and righteous thoughts
Of peace, shall be our path to salvation.
Who among us is brave enough to lay down their arms?
We must stand united for peace
Or die a soldier's death for naught.

Unrhymed Words

Beauty is an easy thing to rhyme; ugly is much harder.
So don't look for rhythm or frilly verse here—
Only the alliteration of hope versus hate,
And man versus God.

The Rotary Prayer

Quoting Ralph Waldo Emerson, with a third stanza added by this author …

"For flowers that bloom about our feet,
Father, we thank Thee.
For tender grass so fresh, so sweet,
Father, we thank Thee.
For the song of bird and hum of bee,
For all things fair we hear or see,
Father in Heaven, we thank Thee.

"For this new morning with its light,
Father, we thank Thee.
For rest and shelter of the night,
Father, we thank Thee.
For health and food, for love and friends,
For everything Thy goodness sends,
Father in heaven, we thank Thee."
(Emerson)

"For those who serve beyond themselves,
For fair goodwill where freedom dwells,
For those who bravely provide our care,
We praise these things,

In common prayer."
(Autrey)

Blades of Destruction and a Song of Hope

The gentle winds of change lay stilled by coarse cutting blades of ignorance.
The bloody swath brings death to the glory of all things past.
The plants of unnurtured seeds grow among the flowers and sweet grass in gardens once revered.

The youthful, erect fingers of hate strike unhealable wounds
While evil deeds of the ignorant kill over-bloomed flowers of prosperity.
This garden of life now grows a generation of prickly weeds,
With the scenes of remembered beauty buried below.

We will one day awaken from the dark dreams of destruction
With visions of Resurrection as promised in books of the long dead:
Our blunt tilling plows turning the dirt of hate to fresh soil and stone,
Yielding a birthing bed for new hope.

Familiar roads and hills layered in failed millenniums will rise to be climbed yet again.
Right must then prevail over the wrongs gone past,
With new seeds fathered, well planted, not blindly cast.

Dark clouds must part for God's heavenly light,
Forgiving past sins of untethered blindness.
Then flowers may again bloom about our feet,

In Emerson's poetic grass, "so fresh, so sweet."

Rise up, righteous farmers, now lead and plant.
Turn under the evil in new furrowed rows.
Pray we become thankful for the creation of life,
And humbly seek the light of eternal
Abundance still promised by God. Amen.

Bitter End

The Hawkers they hawked, and their bombs filled the sky.
Politicians kept talking and spreading the lie.
We could have been saved had we only tried.
God shed bitter tears on the day we all died.

Horizons of clouds, now covered in dirt,
Form mushroom-plumed ashes that poison the earth.
The world may keep spinning and circling the sun,
But life is now vanquished and evil has won.

God gave us a plan and showed us the way.
Now prayers go unanswered to those led astray.
We refused to listen, with evil in hand.
No worship will save us in churches of sand.

Our play is over—no laughter, no clowns.
No hope will sustain us; the curtain is down.
The last act is unfinished, from scripts still unread.
No blessings, no prayers bring hope to the dead.

The screens are all darkened and night fills the days.
Our souls lost forever in a nuclear haze.
The battles are over, no victories are won.
No God's looking down: no Father, no Son.

A Prayer for Salvation

Damn you, casters of news!
Have you nothing to tell?
Your words lie like trash
On the roadsides to hell.
Hatred and murder
Fill the columns each day.
Politicians are lying,
Saying all is okay.

If there's a light in the tunnel,
It shines very dim.
I'll pray for salvation,
But my patience is thin.
The book of Revelations
Now seems very near.
Lord Jesus is weeping,
I'm feeling his tears.

Lord God, please save us
From sin's heavy load.
We've traveled too far,
We've run out of road.
Bring us to light, Lord,
Please show us the path.

Don't put us asunder,
Don't show us your wrath.

Let us kneel and repent,
Pray we soon find our way.
Hands are now folded,
It's past time to pray.
Tomorrow is now,
We've no time to lose.
So join me, my friends,
It's now time to choose.

PART II:
Love & Affection

Rabbits

God's grace keeps us sane,
lest we be like rabbits in the grass.
For me, I'd trade sanity
to lie with you in tall grain.
The thought of our reunion
makes rapid my breath.
I cherish the thought of you and
will until my death.

Dreams

The pillow is the resting place for all my thoughts.
I look across at your pure unblemished face ...
Your soft golden hair caresses my hand with inviting sensations.
I feel the warmth of your skin and embrace the full length of you.
We are like one body, one mind, inseparable souls.

I smell the sweetness of your body and its mystical power.
My heart is full of our now requited love, and I want it to never end.
My mind screams for your affection that only sleep can overcome.

As the sun's golden light awakens me, and I reach for you again,
Your pillow lies untouched because you were never really there . . .

Fantasy

In my mind's eye lies a fantasy that
is denied its due requite.
The thoughts are quite specific,
yet, in reality, find their flight.
What am I to do but wonder
at the beauty of her smile.
Perhaps one day I'll find her,
but unlikely on this night.
Alas, I am denied her touch;
I will never hold her close.
For now I have her in my dreams,
if only for one night.

Ron Autrey

Seeing in the Dark

I'm awake. I do not want to be awake. What time is it?
It must be morning; I can feel the sun's energy on my skin.
It's dark. Of course it's dark; I'm blind.
I fumble with the fan switch. It's off now.
So quiet, no sound, no wind, no rain.
I want the sound; I love the sound.

I am dressed, and hungry.
Coffee … I love coffee.
Blind is okay. I feel everything.
I feel the warmth of the sun, so I know it is there.
I am loved. I know I am loved. I hear it every day.
I feel it every day. I love back. I think I do.

God loves me. My friends love me.
Blind is okay. I have my mom. She loves me.
One day, things will be different.
One day, I will love everyone back. I need the sound.
The sound of two breaths, two beating hearts.
Blind is okay. I can do this. I am loved.

Where the Mountains Touch the Sky

I traveled to the mountaintop where the roadway finds its end.
I peered across the wide expanse where the only sound is wind.
Ten thousand years dance quietly by in the mountains,
Where the mountains touch the sky.

I think of life and what is ahead,
For me and all my clan.
Will life go on when I am gone,
Just another grain of sand.
There's surely more for me and mine,
This can't be all there is.

Perhaps we'll find that things can change,
If we only had more time.
For now, I'll smile and stay the course,
And dance in my mind's eye.
For I have seen what lies ahead,
Where the mountains touch the sky.

Tomorrow brings another day, and I will make it mine.
So come along and dance with me,
There may not be much time.
Let's smile and laugh, stroll hand in hand,
Leave memories where they lie.
We will have all we need each day,

Where the mountains touch the sky.
And when it is done and the angels sing,

Our souls will carry on.
The spirits dance before our eyes
And the birds now sing our songs.
We'll think back on times gone by
And smile at all we shared:
From the heavens to majestic peaks,
Where the mountains touched the sky.

Sea Shadows

Your face is obscured by shades of gray shadows.
Still, I see the radiance that cannot be hidden.
Your flowing hair dances in the ocean breeze like
Seabirds floating in midair.
Each wave collapses with the sound of adoration
For the inspiring beauty of a fair maiden wading its shore.
The mist rising from the rushing white sea-foam
Magically paints the canvas of my dreams.
Your arms, spread open, embrace the life,
The love, and the warmth of the world you create.
Blessed was the day of your birth
And all days patiently waiting your presence.

Rhymes

I wish that I were younger,
Maybe forty or forty-two.
Perhaps if I had more money,
Add a zero, maybe two.
To be a bit better looking
And attractive to someone like you
Would make me far more happy
And maybe not so blue.
If all these things could happen
And I could be with you,
Then life would be so pleasant
For me and maybe you …

Profiles of Beauty

Your shadowed beauty is framed by a golden sky,
Like an image married to the sea.
The rising sun shines a lovely light
And lingers through the day.
You dance along an endless shore
In a scene from life's unfolding play.

If I Were a Sailor

A special boat for me
Would be a wooden schooner
To take me out to sea.
No storm could overtake my course,
No sky could steal my light.
I'll choose the path less traveled
And sail on through the night.
There is a seat beside me;
You fill it if you dare.
My endless love will guide you;
A grand life we could share.
Come quickly to the seashore
And keep your duffel light.
Blue skies and stars await you;
We leave before first light.
Cast off your tribulations,
Grasp my hand and step aboard.
A new life is set before you,
Thanks be to Christ our Lord.
Amen.

The Perfect Ballerina

You are the perfect ballerina in a thousand men's dreams.
Men you will never meet have seen you and breathe in the very thought of you.
You float as an image in the minds of men and women who define beauty and poise
with a mere fleeting memory of having seen you pass by.

You cannot help or hide who you are in the thoughts of others.
Your presence paints an irretrievable portrait of beauty for those yearning
for their own presence and image to be known in the world they live in.

I am, like many others, deeply thankful for the brief moments our lives shared.
My waking thoughts bring a smile because I know that
sometime soon, I will see your lovely face and hear your voice, and touch your hand and heart.

You

I stare out across the water and up into the morning sky:
They embrace the other quietly, like lovers old as time
Dancing on the mirrored surface, reflecting the trees nearby.
My thoughts begin with thankfulness for all I hear and see.
Still my eyes fill quick with aching sadness
That you are not here with me.

A Christmas Wish

For me and for you,
I wish a joyous Christmas Eve
and a pleasant Christmas Day.
With moments of reflection
and fond memories that make you sigh.
And sweet breaths of excitement as you
face the coming year,
with grand aspirations for a life
of love and tender thoughts
to make you smile …

A Birthday Wish to My Wife

In our marriage, as two became one,
The distance of a single night apart became too far.

We joined together in love to celebrate the blessing of your birth.

Know that you are my breath,
You are my beating heart.

Happy birthday!

Love always,
Ron A

Thoughts of You

Who has your heart?
Who do you see
When your eyes close at night?
Are you thinking of me?

The distance makes vague all
Thoughts of your touch.
Do you remember our first moments?
Do you love me that much?

I've something to ask:
Not very big … quite small.
A hug and a kiss,
Or maybe two.
My thoughts are for happiness
For me and for you.

The Eyes Win

Look me in the eyes
And you can clearly see,
My heart follows my desires,
And you are everything to me.

Look me in the eyes
And you will surely know,
I am the one to fill your dreams
With love that only grows.

Look me in the eyes and ask,
Are you in love with me?
The answer lies beyond my voice:
The world is ours to see.

Take my hand and you will know
My heart wants only you.
In your eyes I see your soul
And pray you'll love me too.

I'll hold you close
And count your breaths,
I'll whisper in your ear:

I love you now and always will,
Until my heart is stilled by death.

PART III:
Depression

Word Songs

Soft-flowing words that rhyme
Bring battle to my darkest thoughts.
They flow and ebb in poetic verse,
Spread light and peace of mind.

The rhythm dances in my head
Like music in my ears.
While from my seat I travel
Across both land and time,
My storied life is safe from harm
And all good thoughts are mine.

Dark Clouds of Depression

Dark clouds of depression move silently in the background noise of life.
Then one day, without alarm, the crescendo of darkness rises like a thunderhead
With synaptic lightning strikes and revolting evil images
That push the darkness over the light.
There is no making sense of it; the mind is off its map.
You give it lead and plummet into the depths,
Or pull your sword and thrust your shield against the onslaught of the attack.
This is not good and evil in hand-to-hand.
It is layer upon layer of neurotic decay in a bottomless black abyss.
Face it. Fight it. Do not let it win.

Pain, the Play, Is a Tragic Composition

It writes the words and directs the script
With rhythmic, cruel sedition.
I mind the hurt, my voice complains,
I pray that God will help me.
His answer clear as sky is blue,
He says the pain will heal me.
My puzzled soul did ponder this
And wandered through my thoughts.
With open eyes I came to know
That pain is all around me.
If yours is great, too much to bear,
I'll help you if I can.
The peace for me is in my heart:
God's love is mine to share.

Gray Clouds for Alison

When I was younger, I could see blue sky and golden sunsets.
Now I see clouds, not blue clouds, gray clouds, my gray clouds.
They are always with me.
Sparks of light startle me, sometimes noises scare me.
I look to the sky now and see my thoughts.
I see visions of people and places in refined detail.
I hear the voice in my head; it is my voice.
It is a happy voice and sometimes a sad voice, but it is my voice.
I feel warmth and cold and bedtime snuggles.
I feel love and share love, with warm embraces.
Still, there is a hole in my life, and it is not my gray vision.
My soul needs a partner, my heart needs a home,
A dueling pulse sharing the silence on my pillow.
My loving God knows me and knows my heart's desire.
My soul will marry its rightful partner, and my mind will find peace
And rest in my gray clouds . . .

When I Awaken

When I awaken mornings with a cloud inside my head,
the purpose of the day is fleeting
when at last I leave my bed.

No smiles or pleasant thoughts arise
as the hours pass me by.
I hope the night will find me well
and leave clouds up in the sky.
No time for things unpleasant,
no place for those unkind.
Let's hope the sundown changes
my weak and troubled mind.

Before night turns into morning
with cooing turtledoves,
I'll rest my heart with dreaming
of those I chose to love.

Tomorrow is made for dreamers
and sparkling eyes and wishes.
For you, my love, I'll bless you
with all my love and kisses.

A Troubled Mind

Dark is the day with a troubled mind,
When terror fills the night.
What lies ahead for the punished soul,
With no end in sight.

Lie with me and hold my heart,
Let fears be held at bay.
Embrace me now and through the night,
And in the following day.

Your beauty shines away the dark,
And clears my ailing mind.
Will you love my broken soul?
Can you truly be that kind?

The night is ours
With love to share,
Its pleasures now await us …
So hold me close 'til morning light.
Tomorrow soon will find us.

Ah, Spring!

I want to curl up on the floor
And sleep until the fall.
The shades of winter bore me,
No feelings left at all.

Perhaps the spring will cure me
Or leave me still again.
The bright spring sun lights up the sky,
The wind caresses my skin.

The flowers bloom and gently sing
A dance of newborn leaves.
I'm thankful now I am awake
And dancing in the breeze.

Ron Autrey

Daybreak

My first thoughts are the truest
When the dawn lets the day begin.
Before life rains down and brings the old troubles
Still left to tend.

Old deeds and thoughts
Lined up to fill my day,
Leave little precious time
For new roles to play.

My eyes are closed,
But sleep no longer comes.
I'm forced to wake and rise
Like the morning sun.

Maybe now, maybe never,
I'll put the time at bay
To find a smile and a friend
To share this newfound day.

It's eyes wide open
To the sun shining bright,
To face the world once more,
Until I kiss the coming night.

"He Ain't Right"

Right as rain on a clear sunny day,
Like a bad uncle and what he might say!
I sing like a bullfrog at night in the swamp,
My hobby is counting the ants I then stomp!
So lower your sights and judge me if you must,
I hope I bring laughter from dawn until dusk. He-he-heh.

PART IV:
Thoughts for You

A Wish for You

So many days, your thoughts are filled
With all the things that you must do.
If only I had more time, you say,
Then I would see my work is through.

You must make time for other things;
Your work is never done.
One day you'll see the light grow dim,
You'll see life's setting sun.
It's then you learn that it was more
Than a race you never win.

Live with the time you have each day,
It is all you can truly know.
Find the things which warm your heart,
The friends who help it glow.
It matters not the tasks undone;
No peace can be found there.
Find laughter's love and happiness
Before your setting sun.

And when you pass from this busy life
With no worries, fears, or cares,
All your days will be at peace
With all the time to share.

I pray that day is far away,
But when it finally comes,
There will be no lists, no things undone,
Just beauty, peace, and love.
It is then you'll see the face of God
And know you've finally won.

Summer Thoughts

Heat from the sun, like a furnace to my thoughts,
Brings nothing pleasant to share from my lips.
Parched, with no music left in my voice,
A bitterness fills the day.

Come quickly, fall leaves and gentle, cool breezes.
I'll welcome you with legions of verse.
Bring sea waves that roll softly in early morning light,
Clouds and light winds,
And coolness to the night.
Gold sunsets wink slyly and sink from the sky,
Marking each day as life quickly slips by.

Lord, grant these wishes, and for all days ahead,
Heal hearts that are broken and soothe troubled minds.
I've too much to do
And not enough time.

Morning Over the Lake

The morning scene over the lake is never disappointing. It brings the mind's eye into focus and inspires us toward thoughts outside of the mundane and material world. The lake, sky, and forest present a portrait of the harmony which can exist between Mother Nature and man.

As the sun rises, the geese cackle out a song … a refreshing embrace of the new day. The deer amble and feed in God's garden, and the mama bear and her cubs walk in single file toward their den. The eagle soars above the mist and sees the new day and all its possibilities. I stand on my deck overlooking nature's beauty, and thank God for my existence and the blessings I have been given.

I am, for the moment, in a loving embrace with all I see and hear. I begin the day with new hope that others have shared the same appreciation of this new day. Before I turn the scene toward the harsher world created by man, I offer thanks to my Creator for the breath of life and the ability to see beauty amidst the antithesis of his creation.

Amen.

To Heal a Broken Heart

Hot is the passion of desire,
As cold surrounds disdain.
Heartache is the dying love,
And tears the blood of pain.

Go to sleep, put pain at bay;
The night will heal your wounds.
When darkness leaves, you'll start the day:
Your smile like a flower blooms.

The memories passed and locked away
Like water down the stream.
You'll find new love—I promise this—
The future holds your dream.

So, rise from resting beauty sleep,
A new day has been born.
Your secret is safe and yours to keep;
That page of life was torn.

Embrace the day at every dawn.
It's yours to spend away.
Don't look for love, it will find you.
It follows you each day.

A breeze will blow, a leaf will fall,
You'll see you're not alone.
Turn your head, return the smile,
Your love has found its home.

A Widow's Pain

You cannot hear the sound. It is me banging the furniture with my fist as a hammer. I want to feel the pain. I want it to scream with pain and take my mind away from the pain in my heart. The morning starts with a whisper in my ears, "He is gone, he is not coming back." I am nauseated by the thought of another day with him. I move ahead and into the grey hours that start each day.

I smile and thank my loving friends for their repeated blessings of condolence. They tiptoe cautiously around me as though I might break into a thousand pieces. They should not worry. I am already broken into a thousand pieces. My mind does not wander through the day. It rushes to the core of my soul and wrenches my existence into a puppet-like body with no one holding the strings. I know he told me to be strong. "Do not wallow in grief," he said. "Embrace the life remaining and learn to be happy once again. Do this for me, my love . . ." I fight back the few tears I have remaining. They have been replaced with sorrow and anger. I hold the turmoil inside—I smile, and walk through this day, and the next, and hope and pray that I can hold onto the fringes of my sanity.

I am not ready for memorials. Do not write "In memory of" my beloved departed. I remember him! I remember the warmth of his body against mine and the touch of his hand as we danced through our beautiful life together. I remember his smile and laughter, and his tears. Do not tell me to be strong. I am broken. You cannot put the pieces of our life back together. I will gather the fragments of memories and store them painfully away. Someday I will heal and look at each piece and cry again.

A friend held me today and took my hands in hers and said, "Pray with me." She looked into my tired eyes and said again, "Pray with me now. He would want you to find solace in the blessings of God." We prayed together and I asked God to save me from this horrible abyss—to ease my painful burdens of loss. The dark thoughts of death must not prevail over the love we shared. My husband is in heaven, and his love will be with me now and forever. She prayed aloud, "Through faith in the Father, Son, and Holy Spirit, you will live on this earth with Jesus Christ as your savior. You will touch the hand of God and see the living soul of your loving husband. He will be with you for all the rest of your days on earth and forever in heaven . . . Amen."

A Prayer from Heaven

Blessed is this broken heart,
Lord heal her loving soul.
Give warmth to her cold breath,
And strength to fight the devil's toll.
Pray she will soon find peace,
To soothe her troubled mind.
That your loving hands will hold her
Until the day that she holds mine.
Her faith in God will save her,
And She will know the love of your son.
And when her days are ended
We will be together again as one.
Amen

What Do You Think of When You're Dreaming?

What do you think when you're asleep in your dreams?
Where will you go when free to just leave?
Tall city skylines or shopping malls grand,
Or ten miles from shore,
Beyond sight of land?
When the schedule's all clear and no one answers your ring,
You will know I am gone
And I'll see you in spring.
#Bonefish #Tarpon #Tuna
#PeaceofMind

Night Shades

Shades of the dwindling day fade into the coming night.
The artful glow sinks in the sky as darkness shades the light.
Now rest your soul and tired limbs, let sleep begin its play.
Your dreams and loves await you on your pillow where you lie.
The morning sun will dry the dew and the day will have its start,
and you'll awaken fresh and new with love deep in your heart.
Now face the world with kindness and stow your worried thoughts,
Your purpose is before you and not past battles fought.
Breathe in the day, embrace the light,
And make new smiles and carry them
All day and into the night.

Ronaldo

Night Thoughts

When you rest at night
and see the thoughts deep behind your eyes,
do you see the child that was you,
and is he still there?
Is he happy or sad,
or just lying there?

Hateful Dread of Evil

The hateful dread of evil thought will perish in a fight,
So pray to God for a piercing beam
Of love's empowering light.
Stand tall and rise against your foe,
And stab it as it starts.
This life is yours and yours to save
With Lord Jesus in your heart.

He said I am the way and the light
To find your path back home.
Through me you'll find your peace of mind
And never fight alone.

I'll stop the storm and bring the sun.
You'll feel me hold your hand.
Your soul will beam as love prevails.
You're back on promised land.

Sheathe your blade and take this day;
Your fight has now been won.
We'll fight again and still prevail—
I am the Spirit, the Father, and Son.

Wise Mr. Oak

I had a little chat with Mr. Oak today …
He lives just down the lane.
What wisdom do you have for me:
Can you tell me, will it rain?

He spoke in low tones and grumbled,
As wet as wet we'll be.
I thanked him for the warning.
Is that all you have for me?

His barkened face sagged in a frown,
And I asked what could it be?
He sighed and spoke now clearly,
And said with some disdain,
Next week the market stumbles,
And continues to go down.

All the Time in the World

I must make time for something:
It's most important, I say.
I curse the crowded days aloud
For no one in particular to hear.

It seems I say the same thing
Around this time each year.
So busy, I am chasing things,
My mind is never clear.

One day I'll find the tasks all done,
No letters left to send.
I'll find my everlasting peace
When time has found its end.

Ron Autrey

The Ninth Inning

I'm letting some things go …
You know, stuff I bought
Here and there over the decades.
Things of significant value but still
Just things.

They have value, but not so much to me.
They were simply tools I used to create history
And memories—excitement and laughter ….

That's what hurts. I'm letting old memories slip away.
I used them up, and now they are merely passing thoughts.
But still, when the people and houses and boats and things are all gone,
It's not the material things that I'll miss.
It's the touch, the smile, and occasional hug.

The sadness of seeing what once was, slip away,
And knowing it will never be back again—that is the sadness.
I'll get some new things, but it is much harder now.
Harder to create history, events, and amazing adventures.

With fewer years ahead than all those past,
I look for the little things. Small stuff that brings me a moment
Of pleasantness. I love to write things down.
That brings some relief to the sadness.
Perhaps I will write to you, and you will smile,
Or maybe just be sad along with me. That's okay too.

PART V:
Healing Thoughts

Moonlight, Moon Bright

Moonlight, moon bright,
First moon I see tonight.
Take my heart
And make it whole.
Soothe my pain
And heal my soul.
I look out through the stars,
I see your wondrous sight.
Moonlight, moon bright,
You're my moon tonight.

Ron Autrey

A Child's Prayer

There is a little light you see
when darkness turns to blue.
I stare out at the sky and pray
you can see me too.
I listen to the stars at night
and this is what they say:

"The one you love
can hear you now,
and every thought you pray."
I know you're gone forever
and you're never coming home.
But I remember what Jesus said
when I was all alone.
He said you were no longer dead,
and heaven was your home.

Still, I miss you every day,
and when darkness comes each night,
I stare up into the sky and pray
you will see my light.

"Now I lay me down to sleep,
I pray the Lord my soul to keep.
God, bless Mommy. And God,
please tell Daddy, that little light …
that little light was me."

Virginia in the Flowers

Your mom is now a memory
Of love and smiles so sweet.
The hugs and tears and memories
Are forever yours to keep.

You'll find her in the sunrise,
She will speak to you each day.
You'll find her in the flowers
Smiling up at you to say,
Don't cry for me my darling.
Everything will be okay.

As you walk through the garden
And kneel to smell the rose,
You will find her in the blossoms,
In love's surrounding glow.

Close your eyes and think of her
It's then you'll hear her sing.
You can talk to her when flowers bloom,
Especially in the Spring.

PART VI:
Memory Vignettes

The Tarpit

"Help me! Come now, my foot is stuck in the tar."

My two sisters laughed at first, but then came running. Sandy, my younger sister, grabbed a stick and held out one end.

"Grab it and hold on. I'll pull you out of the tar," she said.

Looking back on the experience, I know it was not a life-threatening event. But for a young boy, it was terrifying, and would become a lifelong memory.

Every child has a memory of some special place—usually a forbidden place. Tallahassee, Florida, was no different. From behind our house, a mysterious tarpit in a large undeveloped area beckoned us. The backyard was fenced with old wood boards and chicken wire. There was no gate, and leaving the backyard was not allowed. The land beyond the fence was sandy soil, scrub oak trees, and palmetto bushes. Still, it held a mysterious lure for me and my younger sister by two years, Sandy. My older sibling was less adventurous, with a standoffish judgmental reserve. The fence was turned up from the bottom on one corner, and we crawled under the ragged steel mesh. We could smell the tar: the unique odor resembled burned crude oil with a dash of vanilla. When the tar got on you or your clothes, it was not coming off.

Beyond the protection of the fence, we stood there in the dangerous place—broken bottles, buckets, old car seats, and discarded appliances cluttered the setting. A cloud of imaginary evils lived in that pit. My sisters and I talked and speculated about what would happen if we walked onto the tar. Surely, we'd sink past our necks and be lost forever. We wondered how many bodies already lay beneath the black muck. We told stories that enhanced the allure of its mystery. Our cousins, Lester and Paul, added color and drama with their renditions of the tales about the tarpit. Lester was the oldest of all of us, but only by a couple of years. He embellished the stories in a way that made the tarpit even more scary. Paul, like my older sister, was a bit less adventurous. He assured us that if we didn't die a horrible death, we would be in really big trouble when Mam Ma (our paternal grandmother) and our parents found out. Mam Ma's life and the stories she told about growing up in Tallahassee could fill at least a dozen books.

"Git back in here, young'uns," Mam Ma would holler from the porch, "and cut me a switch. I'm gonna tan your hides."

I can't remember if she actually swatted us with the mulberry branch, but the threat was enough to motivate us to crawl back through the fence to the safety of the backyard. Away from the tarpit, our adventures continued and we crawled under the house, looking for racoons, possums, and other critters.

The mysteries of the tarpit and other daring adventures lost their intrigue over time. Our life was pleasant and simple, and we were generally content just playing stickball, kickball, and catch. We were still young, and the world ahead was just as mysterious.

Talquin Tales

Like a scene from the 1957 television show *Leave It to Beaver*, the Autrey family car trips were brutally hysterical. The drive to my father's childhood home in Tallahassee provided a script worthy of a sitcom screenplay. In the back seat, Sandy sat on one side of Susan, and I sat on the other. My five-year-old brother Tom sat curled up in the front seat, close to mom. This arrangement limited the chaos and physical interactions but did little to stop us from tormenting each other during the three-hour drive.

The anticipation of a Thanksgiving family reunion was exciting, but I was keenly focused on the big turkey hunt planned for the day before the epic dinner. When we passed the baseball park, where Dad as a young boy used to walk up and down the stadium, selling popcorn, peanuts, and sodas, we knew that we were in the capital city.

It has been more than forty years since those first trips to visit Mam Ma and Pap Pa, but I can still remember the red clay roads, leading up the hill toward the state's capital building. I did not know at the time how rare and memorable those family gatherings would become.

The Autrey house on River Road was a classic Norman Rockwell picture, without the Thomas Kincaid glow. It was a postwar, worn-out, rural Florida setting that represented both my father and his father's family roots, and it became a foundation for my childhood.

The visit always began with a hunting trip to bring home the Thanksgiving turkey. Like men going off to war, Dad and Uncle Clyde cleaned their shotguns and laid out camouflage clothing they had purchased at the local army-navy store. Dad had a Stevens double-barrel shotgun and a Remington .22 caliber automatic rifle with a modern synthetic stock. I had a single-shot .410-gauge shotgun with a wooden stock and hammer-style cocking.

Just holding the gun and the shotgun shells instilled a sense of awe—not power over man or nature, but a feeling that I was included and doing something important. My dad had a gun, I had a gun, and we were going hunting. Even at a young age, I always felt as though I was part of a story that was unfolding daily. I was the character and the author, and each page was a new and exciting experience recorded in my young mind.

Upon reaching our destination we parked the car and quietly pushed the car doors closed. Any noise would scare the turkeys, and the morning hunt would be lost. It was cold and dark, and my hands seemed to freeze on the steel barrel of my gun. I could see my breath.

"Follow me and stay close. Walk on the edge of your feet and you won't make as much noise," my dad told me in a stern voice. "Keep your barrel up, or you'll get dirt in it, and don't load your gun until I tell you."

I had hunted with my dad before, but not in the woods. On a farm near our home, we hunted doves in an open field. I killed my first dove in flight with a crossing shot from my shotgun. I remember how good it felt when he bragged to the other hunters about my newfound shooting skills. Knowing that my dad was proud of me was a feeling I would covet for many years to come.

The ground was wet and covered with autumn leaves. I tiptoed and struggled to keep up with my dad. Twigs snapped under my feet, and it seemed so loud I thought every animal in the forest heard me. I was afraid, but not from the darkness or wondering what was ahead. My fear was that I would disappoint my dad.

We walked for fifteen minutes and climbed over a barbed wire fence line (I learned how to do this properly while on the dove-hunting trips at the farm). In the darkness before sunrise, I could barely see the treetops and the squirrel nests, but I could hear them barking and scurrying from branch to branch. The squirrels would not be hard to hit—not like a dove.

Dad whispered, "Sit by this tree and don't move. You can shoot after the sun begins to rise. I'm going to be over there."

He pointed his gun in the direction of a pathway down the fence line.

"If you need me, shoot three times in the air." Dad spoke softly but with a clear and concise message. "Don't shoot level. Always shoot up."

His directness was at times frustrating, but I always knew what was expected. He quietly slipped away until I could no longer see him. As he walked toward the fence line, into the darkness, and I was alone in the dark woods of Wakulla Forest.

There was an eerie stillness in the air and my breathing was the only sound. The temperature felt colder than when we first got out of the car. I fiddled with my gun, practicing with the hammer. Pulling the hammer back was very hard, and my fingers were cold. The gun could go off if you let the hammer go before it locked. I checked and rechecked my pocket for the shells. Number 7½ for squirrels, number 4 for turkeys . . . and I had one shell with a lead slug, in case I saw a deer or a hog. I was not troubled by any doubtful thoughts about what I might do when it was time to shoot. The lessons I had learned from my dad were larger than the simple details of aiming and shooting. The obscure qualities of self-confidence and determination were handed to me by my father. I was ready.

Pop.

My dad would surely hear the sound of the .410 shot. I had killed my first squirrel. I thought my dad would think I had fired the gun accidentally. *No, it was a squirrel,* I hoped he would say to himself. I understood how my dad, the hunter, thought about the hunt. He had seen the turkeys drop down from their roost. It would take nearly twenty minutes to get within range by belly-crawling along the fence line. The turkeys hopped one by one over a sandy knoll. Dad could see the hens and drakes, but not the big tom turkey he had spotted while scouting the area a day earlier.

Pop.

Another .410 report from my gun. It had not been that long since the last shot. Dad would be thinking; *Is he signaling? No, he must be alright. He is just shooting at a squirrel.* The big tom turkey cautiously stuck his head into the opening. His neck appeared and then he pulled back. After a few seconds, the turkey stepped into the clearing along the fence and hopped over the knoll. His beard hung majestically like a medal of triumph. Dad crawled patiently and edged closer to the bottom that held the turkeys.

The turkeys would hop back over the knoll one by one. Dad waited patiently, but the big tom didn't come back over. Had the gunshots spooked the big male turkey? Dad waited thirty seconds . . . then a minute. He could take a smaller bird, but the big gobbler had to be coming. Then the gobbler hopped into the clearing—

twenty pounds of proud turkey with its tail feathers spread out like a large colorful fan. The 16-gauge shotgun pounded the bird with number 4 lead balls, and the turkey fell in his tracks. Now, without thoughts of work or shop or family, Dad's heart was beating fast as he scrambled over to his kill. It was a fine turkey with a nine-inch beard and long spurs protruding from the back of his thick scaly legs.

Pop.

The .410 fired again, and Dad became more concerned. *Time to go he thought,* and returned to the tree where he had left me. He saw the two squirrels I had killed, but I was not there. He looked around and called out. I had moved to another tree deeper into the woods. I looked back at the dimly lit forest, and the trees all looked alike. I walked quickly to another familiar looking tree, but there no squirrels. I was lost. I wasn't afraid. I knew my dad would find me—at least I hoped that he would, before the bears did.

I waited nervously and after what seemed like a very long time, I could hear Dad coming. Holding the prize turkey by the feet, over his shoulder. He came quickly, almost running toward me. He looked down at me and I felt the simultaneous emotions of guilt and relief sweep over me.

"Gather up your squirrels and gun, it's time to go," was all he said.

I remember how proud I was to have him as a father. I was happy he killed the turkey, and even happier he found me in the woods. My father did not waste time criticizing me for getting lost, instead, he told me how proud he was of my bounty of squirrels. I still felt bad about getting lost in the woods, and remember thinking, *One day, I want to be the one to kill the turkey.*

My mind still wanders back to that day, turkey hunting in Wakulla State Forest, and what my father was thinking as he trampled through those woods. He was raised just above poverty level and determined to reach new heights to provide for his family. I was sure he wanted just a *little* more than we needed. Not billions, but enough to get everything he could out of life. I *knew* he would be the one to find and harvest the Thanksgiving turkey. In my eyes he was incapable of failing. He was a driven man and rose to the top of every situation, with little patience for anything other than success.

Back at the house, he walked to the side door and stepped into the kitchen.

"Good Lord," Mam Ma said. "Pap Pa, come look what a turkey Buck has."

Pap Pa was sitting in his living room chair, soaking his feet. He stood slowly and walked to the kitchen doorway and said, "Son, that's a big gobbler. Where'd you shoot him?"

After Dad's reply, Uncle Clyde chuckled and asked, "You weren't on the posted side of that fence, were you?"

I watched Mam Ma pull up a stool next to a galvanized metal washtub, where she would skin and clean the squirrels.

"You boys better get cleaned up for dinner," she said.

Thanksgiving dinner featured two turkeys that year. I can still taste the difference between a store-bought bird and the wild taste of the Wakulla Springs turkey. The difference represented more than just how the two birds tasted. It was about a story of a father and son venturing into the woods to show each other, and everyone else, that we were providers and winners in the game of life.

That Thanksgiving Day was a memorable family celebration. It would be the last time in more than forty years that I would enjoy the experience of hunting in the Wakulla Forest with my dad.

The Isle of Palms

"I do not want to move!"

My not-so-happy ten-year-old sister, Susan, sat stubbornly under the keyboard of an old upright piano. She furiously scribbled her objections on the exposed wooden underside of the piano. Susan and I both wondered if she might even change my parent's minds about moving. Although, Sandy and I anxiously looked forward to the moving adventure. At the time, Tom was only five years old and more concerned about whether Mom was making cookies that day. I can still see the image of him clinging to my mother's apron.

My childhood memories of the Autrey family home in Jacksonville are a rich part of my life. It was the starting place for what would become a phenomenal ride through the "American Dream." I can vividly recall the sound of the fall winds rushing through the tall pines, the winter storms would shape them into beautiful ice sculptures. As a young boy, I strolled up and down the rows of vegetables and luscious strawberries that filled the garden in springtime. The vacant land between our house and my mother's family home was a place to run, play, and roll around in the pine straw. Looking back on that time, I can see myself in that small Riverview neighborhood, looking up at the tall trees and into the blue sky. I was happy and blessed with the freedom to dream.

Before moving from our Northside home, while fishing in a small boat with my grandfather and grandmother, I hooked a large redfish under the Trout River bridge. Every fisherman has a tale about the "one that got away." It the first of what would become a lifetime of fishing experiences for me. I did not land that first fish, but I remembered its golden color and the penny-sized black spot on the tail as it rolled away from the boat. Seeing my disappointment, grandaddy knowingly assured me that there would be plenty more fish to catch.

I remember, on the evening of our last Christmas before moving, walking with my dad to the top of the hill above the house. Dad used a telescope to show us a world that was bigger than we imagined. From that elevated position we could see the moon over the Atlantic Ocean. As I looked in the telescope's lens at the starlit sky, I felt small, like a pebble of sand on an endless beach. That night marked the beginning of a new chapter for me and our family.

In 1961, we made the life-altering move from the northside neighborhood of Riverview to a modern new world in Jacksonville Beach. Though I was leaving behind the first nine years of my life, I would keep my childhood memories for a lifetime. Walking past the large ominous sand hills on the way to H. F. Kite Elementary School was a daily adventure. I will never forget catching blue crabs with a string and a chicken leg under the Trout River bridge with my granddaddy Roy White.

At the time, I did not consider or understand that my mother was also leaving her childhood home. I can see now that leaving behind the closeness of the family compound was a major milestone in her life as well. Like my dad, she was also looking forward to a new and more prosperous life for our family. My mother was always thinking about her children first. She made sacrifices and fought battles that we never knew about. I do believe that if you see a happy child, you will find a mother that made it happen.

I would miss my third-grade teacher, Mrs. Rose. I loved her and brought her deposit drink bottles as gifts. They were as good as money at the gas station next to my school on Lem Turner Road. I would also continue to long for the mysterious girl that lived on the other side of the tall backyard fence at my grandparents' house. We touched our hands together through the mesh wire fence. It was a very special moment for me. I often wonder where she is now, and if she remembers our meetings at that fence. With her beautiful perfect face and long dark hair, she was unlike anyone I had ever encountered. We never spoke a word but I will never forget her.

Moving was like a fantastic dream. We would live in a brand-new house on a small river, near the Atlantic Ocean. Being on the water would bring new and exciting activities to our daily lives. After a final goodbye to our northside home, we made the hour-long drive on the old Beach Road to our new Isle of Palms paradise. It was a beautiful ranch-style home on Silver Palm Drive. The street names in the neighborhood would soon be like chapters in a new book of living for me. We had a large backyard with a pool. The house was within rowing distance of the Intracoastal Waterway. The endless woods and marshes in North Florida provided new opportunities for hunting and fishing with my dad. It was the start of a new life of adventure. I said goodbye to my fourth-grade friends and hello to a brand new Seabreeze Elementary School in Jacksonville Beach.

In the year before moving to the beach, my dad built a twelve-foot-long wooden rowboat in the living room of our house and brought it to our new waterfront home. Very soon after settling in, we were fishing from our dock on the canal behind the house. We had cane poles and bread balls and quickly mastered the art of mullet fishing. The experience was unifying for our family, everyone loved living on the water. The fishing added another level of excitement and intrigue to my life, I never knew what would be on the other end of my line.

In the summer of 1962, the first friend I made was Archie Lee. He lived three streets away on Royal Palm Drive, and we remained friends for the five decades that followed. One beautiful spring morning, Archie paddled from his canal to ours in his father's heavy 14-foot-long rowboat and we rowed to the easternmost canal. We had live shrimp left over from his father's fishing trip the previous day. I had my dad's oversized fishing rod that was designed for fishing on the ocean for large kingfish and giant grouper.

We were barely set with the anchor, when I cast a long distance to the marshy corner where the outflow of a small tributary poured into the canal. The red-and-white cork settled upright and was immediately yanked straight under. I set the hook and knew my world was about to change for the better. After a few minutes of battle with the strong fish, we netted a 10-pound red bass. It was the biggest fish either of us had ever seen up close. Archie's excitement was contagious. He made me feel like I had done something important; something amazing. It was a very good feeling and, this time, the big fish did not get away.

We pulled up the boat anchor and returned to my house. The giant red bass was kept fresh in a cooler with ice, until my dad could get home and see what a prize I had caught. I can imagine the pride he must have felt upon seeing such a great fish. Many years later, I felt the same way about my son and grandson, and the many fish that they caught in the same waterways. My dad taught me most of what I know about fishing. The lessons I learned with his guidance, along with the wonderful outdoor experiences we shared, shaped me into the man I am today.

One of the best fishing spots was just a short walk from our house to a neighbor's dock. George Whitehurst was a nice man who knew a lot about fishing. We caught speckled trout from his dock with just a mirror lure plug. My dad once caught a record sized flounder off George's dock. George and Evelyn Whitehurst became my mom and dad's best lifelong friends. Knowing that I brought the two families together, gave me a sense of pride and accomplishment. Being new to the Isle of Palms and not knowing anyone there, my mom and dad found George and Evelyn to be a Godsent blessing.

Rowboats gave way to a seventeen-foot fiberglass boat with high sides, and a huge Evinrude outboard engine. That boat could take us up the river to the Atlantic Ocean. My dad learned to catch the larger species of fish including king mackerel, giant redfish, and black drum. We caught sheepshead with hand-caught fiddler crabs. It was my granddaddy's specialty. He and Dad would laugh out loud, as they watched me running in circles on the marsh flats along the intracoastal waterway. I scooped up the nickel-sized fiddler crabs in my hand and winced in pain at the bite from their small, but powerful, pincher claws. I knew that they were not laughing at me. It was more like an exuberant expression of how happy they both were with the experience of being together as a family, boating and fishing on the beautiful North Florida waterways.

My dad's life was filled with the challenges of building a career in business while raising a family in the turbulent sixties.

My granddad's guidance, along with my dad's love for my mother, brought them to Jacksonville to start a family. Dad began his working life at the bottom and worked his way up to the top in a lifelong business career. His success would filter down to the future generations of his children and grandchildren.

One Sunday morning, after dressing for Sunday school and church, I slipped away to a nearby canal behind our house. I wanted to try a new fishing method, using live shrimp and a simple fiberglass pole, with just a hook, a short length of line. I salvaged the last four live shrimp from the dock's bait bucket, and headed out across the sandlots to my special fishing spot. Within seconds, the first shrimp provided an excellent speckled trout. The second bait landed a flounder of decent size, and the third was a black drum. The fourth shrimp brought a strike that broke my line. I will never forget that morning. I felt like a winner, and it was a good feeling. I made it back to the house in time to leave for church. In my prayers I said, "Thank you, Lord, for my life and this great morning."

Some of the many fond memories of fishing with my dad took place in Pablo Creek. In the afternoon when he got home from work, we would run our small boat way up Pablo Creek and into the cypress swamps of the Dee Dot Ranch. The Creek changes from saltwater to freshwater as you travel away from the river's main channel. It was home to more alligators than the Alligator Farm in St. Augustine, Florida.

We fly-fished using small green frog poppers and found freshwater black bass under every old cypress stump we passed by as we drifted with the tide. In the colder winter months, we trolled the channels of the Intracoastal Waterway for speckled trout and hunted green-winged teal ducks in the marshy edges of the river's tributaries. The time we spent together gave me the opportunity to bond with my dad on a personal level. It is very likely that he learned as much about me as I did about him on our many fishing trips.

There were several other boats in our family yearbooks, but the 16-foot, unsinkable tri-hull was central to many family memories. Though it sank twice at the dock in the Isle of Palms, the boat provided a platform for fishing and water skiing on Lake Johnson in Keystone Heights. We had nice houses on Lake Johnson and later on Lake Geneva, but the first accommodation was a rented Quonset hut type trailer. It was a place where we could take refuge from a busy complex world, and relax and live a simple and enjoyable way of life. The whole family loved spending time at the lake. We spent countless summer weekends on the lakes in Keystone Heights. As a family, we fished, skied, and barbecued, while growing up together in the nineteen sixties.

The early years of boating and camping with my family gave me a lasting appreciation of the beauty of nature. It also taught me the personal skills of self-reliance and confidence. I saw challenges not as problems, but as adventures in life and how to live it to the fullest measure of success and enjoyment. While the importance of personal development and relationships was significant, I also learned that enjoyment often comes with a financial burden. As a teenager, I began to feel the pressure of my future obligations to achieve my own success.

The fourteen years we lived on Silver Palm Drive shaped my life in many positive ways. My siblings and I joined the other neighborhood kids to make up the squads for seasonal sports that we played in the neighborhood. We played baseball on the side of the interstate highway, until we were strong enough to reach the cars with a well hit home run. The years that followed put each of us on different paths, but we would always have fond memories of our time together in the Isle of Palms.

With some difficulty, I worked through pre-pubescence and puberty, somehow avoiding the pitfalls that befell some of my friends. I think my shy personality around girls at the time was both an asset and a fault. Lori Del Fonse (1963) was my first love. Lori represents the first time that I saw a girl as something more than a sibling or a team-mate. She was beautiful, and mysterious. My thoughts of her brought on new and unfamiliar emotions. Others would follow, but Lori will always have a special place in my memories.

By the sixth grade, I was raking and bagging roadside clippings to make soft landing bags for a pole-vaulting pit. My daring attempts to fly over a horizontal bar too high to simply jump over was with a ten-foot length of Calcutta bamboo stalk. Later, I discovered that our pool cleaning net had a longer aluminum pole that would hold my weight for even greater heights. My success in the sport came at a good time and helped me to overcome feelings of self-doubt. Pole-vaulting was also beneficial to me through high school and also provided an athletic scholarship to Western Carolina University.

After a short-lived career in Little League baseball and golf, I found surfing. My first surfboard was a memorable chunk of two thick, heavy sheets of plywood glued together and roughly shaped into a crude surfing platform. I begged for that plywood behemoth. Dad must have known it would never provide the buoyancy needed for actual surfing, but he gave in to my persistence and let me find out on my own. Dad was right about his prediction. The heavy board did not float well and caused more injuries than pleasure. Being wrong was another important lesson learned for me.

Many iconic surfboard brands and great memories followed me through my high school and college years. When I wasn't fishing from the Jacksonville Beach Pier, I was surfing the breaking waves around it. I survived John F. Kennedy's assassination, the Beatles, and true love in the fifth, sixth, ninth, and tenth grades. In the summer of 1972, I returned home from college to an empty house. This was not unusual, and I assumed that everyone had gone to the lake house.

I was standing on the floating dock that my dad and I built together, thinking about my life and the unsettling thoughts of my future and the year ahead. In the fall I would be leaving Western Carolina to begin my junior year at Stetson University in Deland, Florida. While marginally qualified for the challenging new curriculum, I changed my academic major to chemistry and had hopes of attending medical school after graduation. The pressure to succeed academically and attend medical school was daunting.

Susan came out to the dock and the expression on her face as she was looking down towards where I was standing told me something was seriously wrong. She said that our grandfather "Pap Pa", had died. Any family death was of course tragic, but this was my first experience with the death of anyone known to me. This new emotion overshadowed my thoughts about school. Pap Pa's Death was so surprising and final. It helped to give me a much broader perspective on what was truly important in life. I try to remember my father's reaction to the death of his father, but it is still a blurry recollection.

As tough as Dad's relationship with his father may have been in his younger years, I know he loved him and cherished their time together fishing and hunting in Tallahassee. I never heard my dad talk about his father until much later in life. Though it might not have been expressed often, I'm sure my grandfather was very proud of my dad and all he had accomplished. I watched my dad successfully grow his business career. I was with him in the early years of near poverty, and he carried us to heights of success that none of us ever dreamed possible.

As tremendous as our lives became, it also added stress to my own journey. Failure was no longer an option for me. Dad never told me directly what career to pursue, and he gave me the freedom to choose my path and to make my own mistakes; and I made plenty of them. I did not gain entry into any medical schools. The unbearable feelings of guilt and failure pushed me to add distance to my problems and I enlisted in the United States Army.

Now the sound of my grandfather's crusty old sawmill voice was gone. The short sage proverbs of wisdom from Pap Pa would no longer fill the rooms of the old clapboard house in the clay hills of Florida's capital city. He lives on in the hearts and memories of everyone who knew him.

I can still see him sitting upright in his chair with both feet soaking in a roasting pot full of warm salt water, hollering to Mam Ma in kitchen.

"Where's my iced tea, woman?"

Chang's Scarlet Rose

Chang screamed, "Oh Grandmama!"

He looked at his leg, blood had already begun to seep down his ankle onto his sandaled foot. Tears filled his eyes as he pulled the thorny branch away from his leg. While the sight of his own blood may have presented him with a valuable lesson, the moment was more painful than developmental. He was crying as he ran to his grandmother, who took him in her arms to sooth the pain away. Chang wanted to return to the garden and destroy the weed that had hurt him.

Chang's grandmother held him close. He gradually slowed his breathing, as the warmth of her skin and soothing voice calmed his pain and anger. She explained that it was not a weed that had caused him the painful scratch. They returned to the garden and she showed him the rose bush, with its prickly thorns, that had caused him to bleed. His grandmother carefully held the bud of a rose in her hand and explained that one day soon, the thorny bush would bloom with many beautiful flowers. He doubted that a skinny, prickly, offensive plant would yield beautiful flowers. It was a subtle lesson for Chang that laid a foundation for future conflicts in life that would yield both pain and beauty.

In the spring of that year, the offensive plants grew taller and the rosebuds turned into flowers. The Crimson Glory roses were so big and beautiful that neighbors and friends came by to see the beautiful garden. It was filled with white and red roses and other beautiful flowering plants.

Chang could now see what his grandmother had promised. He quickly came to love the beauty of the garden. He named his favorite rosebush "Scarlet." His now-healed wound connected him emotionally to the well-being and beauty of the roses in his grandmother's garden. He visited the flowers every day. His grandmother told him that he could talk to the roses, and that while they would not speak back to him, they would surely hear his caring words. She assured him that "Scarlet" would blossom into one of Mount Airy's most beautiful rosebushes.

Friends of Chang's grandmother encouraged her to enter the roses in the *Garden Flowers Contest* at the North Carolina State Fair. The contest was for the biggest and most beautiful roses in the entire state. She explained that she had been growing roses since she was a young woman and didn't have to prove to anyone that her roses were the most beautiful. Everyone knew this was true, and living nearby and growing up with the beauty of the garden made it an important part of their lives. This was especially true for Chang. His first outdoor experiences were in his grandmother's garden. His youthful make-believe adventures played out in the rows of bushes with birds and butterflies following his daring make-believe quests.

The notion of a beauty contest for roses was foreign to Chang. He did however understand the concept of winning and losing. Whether it was running a foot race or shooting baskets, he knew enough to understand that winning was far better than losing. He was convinced that he and his lovely Scarlet Rose would win the contest.

Two months before the big day, Chang was contemplating his victory, as he thoughtfully cared for the roses. He played school sports and lived the normal life of a young boy, but the garden was different. It was a visible and tangible part of his life. Working in the garden side by side with his grandmother forged a loving bond that gave him confidence and feelings of importance.

To everyone's surprise, Chang would have unexpected competition at the state fair. A new neighbor moved into the large estate home at the end of his street. They caused a stir with all the trucks and heavy equipment. The normally quiet neighborhood was now busy and noisy as landscape workers hauled in dirt by the truckload. They uprooted trees and plants and made a massive mess of things.

Chang was curious and monitored the progress from the branch of a large tree overlooking the surrounding fence and into the rear yard of the estate. He watched the trucks unload the soil and plants. The workers were creating a garden, and he could see the bushes with their bases wrapped in burlap. They planted them in neat rows and Chang could see that they already had blooming red and white flowers. Chang thought, *How could this be*? He felt the strong emotions of unfairness. He knew how much work and love his grandmother had put into their garden. He struggled with his confusing feelings of sadness and anger.

Nobody seemed to like the new neighbors. They came in and took charge like they owned the whole town. Rumors were flying. Some people said the man who bought the big house had been to prison. Others said he might still go to jail for embezzling money from investors in his devious business schemes. Shortly after moving in, the new residents began rapidly renovating the old

Victorian house, while landscape workers planted a large and elaborate garden in the rear yard of the estate property.

Chang was now worried that the new competition would spoil his plans for victory. His grandmother consoled him with fresh baked cookies and tried to explain that the contest was not as important as he now thought it had become. Chang was also disappointed in his own feelings. There was no outlet for his growing frustration. Maybe his grandmother was right; winning a contest at the State Fair was not that important. He also knew that he wanted to win, and that the possibility of losing was very troubling.

As the State Fair and the best rose contest approached, Chang's only thoughts were that he had to win the fair's blue ribbon for the biggest and most beautiful rose. On an early summer morning, Chang and his grandmother went into the garden to care for the beautiful roses. He was stunned by the sight of large red petals on the ground at the base of his favorite rosebush. Chang's grandmother pulled him close and hugged him, calmly telling him not to worry, that it was okay for a few petals to fall off the roses. But the next day and for several days that followed, more petals fell. He hated the feelings of dread and the potential loss of his prized scarlet rose. He thought to himself, *Was this my fault? Have I done something wrong? Maybe someone is poisoning the roses!*

What Chang did not know was that the water supply from the community well was being siphoned off by the new neighbor's big garden at the end of the street.

But Chang was determined. After learning about the problems with the well, he carried water in buckets that he collected from the houses of his friends and neighbors. He worked tirelessly to save the roses and tried to keep his hopes up for the big contest. The neighbors cheered his efforts and care for the roses. As the big day approached, he could see that something was wrong. Was it poison in the ground, the air, or water? Could someone be sneaking into the garden and pulling off the beautiful petals? Unfairness and anger flooded his thoughts. His dream of winning the contest was dying along with the roses.

Encouraged by the love and support of his family and friends, Chang stayed in the contest. Chang and his grandmother stood on the porch overlooking the once beautiful rows of flowers. She held him close and wiped the tears from his eyes.

With her hands on Chang's shoulders, she said to him, "My dear Chang, you will have many contests in your life, and you will not win all of them. You can learn from your victories, and your losses. How you respond to your experiences will be what makes you the wonderful man I know you will become."

Even with the missing petals, he thought his scarlet rose might somehow still win. Except for the one new entrant, the competition was not so fierce. The roses in the new neighbor's garden were not even grown here. The bushes were transplanted from a big fancy nursery up north. To Chang, it all seemed so unfair. His grandmother's garden has been producing beautiful flowers for many years. Knowing very little about cultivating roses, the new neighbor simply spent large amounts of money on store-bought plants in a garden that was only a few weeks old.

Chang's beautiful scarlet rose did not win the blue ribbon. The lack of water in his garden had taken too many petals. Although still beautiful to Chang, his roses could not compete with the hothouse roses brought in to defeat him. He clenched his fists and gritted his teeth, trying unsuccessfully to put his emotions aside. He stood at the edge of the garden and fought to hold back the tears.

Chang's grandmother came to him and held him, whispering softly, "I know you are angry. I promise that those feelings will pass. I am so proud of you. Your friends and all the neighbors respect you for what you have accomplished."

She told him that there would be many more roses, and that no contest could ever take away the beauty that he had helped create.

As the memory of the big State Fair faded away, the autumn season brought out the beauty of the sleepy town of Mount Airy, North Carolina. The garden at Chang's grandmother's house was in full bloom. The thorny branches that once painfully branded Chang's youthful skin, now stood as guardians of the biggest and most beautiful roses in all their crimson glory.

The seasons passed one by one, and the love and support Chang had known his whole life stayed with him. He learned that every day was a blessing, and that real prizes in life came not from state fairs or big contests, but from the love and support of his family, and from God in all his glory in the natural beauty of the world.

Written by Ron Autrey for Alex Sink – December 2010

The Meaning of Life

While I have no recollection of the physical trauma of my premature birth, I can imagine that the combination of a gasping blue face and the jaundiced skin of a four-pound newborn was not a pleasant sight for my parents, or the attending medical professionals.

I was born in 1952 and my life expectancy was measured in minutes, not decades. The immediate challenges were clear. Breathing was the struggle but living was the goal. I am forever grateful for the bold actions of the young physician attending to my birth (Dr. Richard Skinner). The unprecedented manual inflation of my collapsed lungs brought life-giving oxygen to my rapidly failing body.

As I grew older, the struggles changed as often as the goals I set for myself. Things like meaning and purpose would come much later. As a young boy, I was given a chance to live and every day unfolded like a story for me. The pages in life recorded one adventurous experience after another. From a seashell against my ear, I could hear another world, and in my mind, I saw myself in a thousand roles and places.

I survived childhood and a colorful adolescence. In high school, I found talent in many sports that carried me through to graduation and acceptance to college. In the four years that followed, I changed universities as often as my academic major. As a premed student, I failed to gain admittance to medical school.

This action alone may have saved countless lives from my substandard abilities as a clinician.

After a brief but meaningful tour in the U.S. Army, I found employment in my father's electrical construction business. Fortunately for me and my family, it was a good fit. I achieved great success throughout my 45-year career. Later in life, with most of my efforts recorded as victories and losses, I reflect fondly on my experiences and what I have achieved. I also think about my own failures and what other outcomes might have been possible. That question remains unanswered for me.

With more of my life behind me than in the days ahead, I am the husband of a loving and caring wife, and the father of three children that I deeply love. I have four wonderful grandchildren, who are just beginning their own journeys. I pray that they will find success in their endeavors and some acceptable level of happiness.

I recognize the infinite complexity of our physical world and wonder endlessly about our ethereal connection with the unknown. For me, I rely on faith in an almighty God. Still, some questions remain unanswered. Are we moved from one circumstance to another by mere chance, or is there a predetermined destiny for each of us? I believe we follow a self-determined plan of travel through life. God's over-arching plan for our lives is altered by our own actions, and those of other people and situations we encounter along the way. Despite my own good intentions, I have found myself lost and literally on my knees asking God to forgive me for my failings, and to guide and help me in my journey through life.

Understanding concepts as nebulous as the holy trinity of God the father, the son, and holy ghost, is a challenge for laymen and clerics alike. In my business career, I discovered that complex intangible concepts can often be defined by their absence. I saw that the absence of leadership brings chaos. The loss of good health can bring tragedy and death. We have all experienced or witnessed the misery that comes from poor health.

We read in the Bible that the absence of good leaves space for evil. One looks at the world around us and evil can be seen where a Godly and moral religion is not revered by the people. For me, living a spiritual life means bringing good into the world through thoughts, words, and deeds. I believe that we are meant to share joy and happiness with ourselves and with others.

I am amazed at the power of a smiling face, and the touch of the hand of a friend on my shoulder. Kind words have often provided me a pathway to avoid despair and hopelessness. In my journey through life, I have seen the mission that God presents to us. When we see pain, we should bring relief. Where there is hunger, bring food. When I see suffering, I bring hope and relief when I am able. It has become clear to me that we must give love in order to receive it. Lifting others up in their time of need will bring blessings from others when I am in despair. I know these things to be true.

The scriptures tell us to take care of our physical body and feed our soul with good thoughts and deeds. When others join or cross my path, I tell myself that they are also fulfilling their purpose in life. I hope to achieve a greater level of understanding and awareness about our journey and the world we live in. Together, we must advance as a society toward peaceful, loving, and productive lives, while passing down the lessons learned from our journey. Our success as caretakers of the blessing of life is the only path that can bring people, states, and nations together in peace and prosperity.

I dream of a world without war, and without suffering and hopelessness. A place where children find only smiles and laughter and families live happily and safely in their home, at peace with the world around them.

I will hold your hand, as you would mine, when your soul passes from the physical body. We will one day be spiritually joined and seated in the heavenly house of our maker. It is then that we will be washed in the light of understanding our purpose, and the true meaning of life.

Until then, let us do good things and think good thoughts. Bringing happiness to others will serve us well in our journey together.

Melisa's Last Dance

My arms yearn to arc majestically above my head, my toes long for the whirl of a pirouette. Yet here I am, dying in my bed, and there is nothing I can do about it. I cannot ignore it; no one wishes to talk about it and I cannot get over the growing frustration of not knowing what day will be my last. My mind is still on the stage in the wedding dance and pas de deux for the fairy king and queen, Oberon and Titania. I know that I am old, I feel trapped in this aging body. I still have vivid thoughts and dreams of music, dance, and laughter. This is not fair. This bed is my prison. I want to hear the music, the applause, and feel my feet against the floor. Is this really the end, the final curtain. Surely there is more for me to do.

I was twenty-five when I danced as the prima ballerina in the New York City Ballet. New York was a different place in the fifties. The dazzling neon lights of Times Square illuminated a flourishing scene of the art and music of the "Beat Generation". We performed in all the major American cities and presented our ballet troupe to the world on the first color television shows. Our European debut included performances on the historically romantic stages in Paris, Rome, and Munich. I miss the glare of the spotlight, the comradery of our corps de ballet, and the sweat and exhaustion of endless travel.

Back in New York, Conrad Ludlow and I performed flawlessly in Balanchine's *A Midsummer Night's Dream*. I close my eyes, and hear Mendelssohn's "Overtures to Athalia," and "The

Fair Melusine." My body painfully tries to sway to the sounds of a dozen violins playing in my head. I can see the Children's Corp in a slow waltz step and brush movement, flowing across the stage, as the symphony plays the calming notes of the "Son and Stranger."

I remember the blurring storm of turbulent upheavals as classical works gave way to music of the "Me Generation." The 1960s collided with my world, and the headlines moved to the sensations of the civil rights movement, and the outlandish sexual revolution. The classical way of life and its music and dance collided with the revolutionary spirit of that generation. The noise of it all overshadowed the fine arts and ballet world. My audience was slipping away, long before I was ready to make a final bow.

After dancing in more ballets than my sexagenarian age, I left the spotlights and retired. In 1973, I left New York City wearing the Handel Medallion given to me by Mayor John Lindsay. To receive the city's most prestigious award for cultural contributions, softened the feeling of finality that came with my departure from the world's stage. I never left the ballet. After moving to Seattle, teaching became my new passion. I published books for dancers with exercises for dancing with grace and beauty. I returned to New York and opened my own ballet school. The legacy and sparkling virtuosity of Balanchine and Prokovsky must be preserved and passed to new generations of dancers.

Now my poor health has taken center stage. While I have much more to do, I am afraid that despite my plans, I will be done. Georgi's spectacular marriage of ballet with acrobatic twists and turns must carry on without my form. The value of my contributions will fill an obituary. Will the books I have written find a new audience or linger in the darkest corners of the very best libraries. Surely my students in Seattle and New York will carry my memory and display all that I have taught them. Or perhaps they will remember me for a short while before I slip into anonymity.

The funeral production may assuage my family's grief, but what about me? I didn't choose to die. I lie here fighting a losing battle inside my cancerous body, but my mind refuses to give up the journey. What right has this cancer to take over my life? Surely God condemns the cruelty of such an unwarranted disease.

I have loved and been loved and danced on the world's stage. The sounds I now hear are nothing like the thunderous applause of ten thousand people standing and cheering, as I bow and kiss the air. The inner peace that many speak of in their terminal moments is beyond my grasp. The music has been replaced with the arpeggio of monotone notes, clicking and whirring in the medical tools at my bedside.

My dearest husband Donald whispers in my ear, "I am here my dearest Millie. I love you. I will always love you."

I do not want to cry—I bite my lip and squeeze his hand tightly. Inside I am quivering, not from pain but rage! I want to scream, "Save me from this insidious disease!"

I can already see and hear my friends speaking kindly of me in the ceremony of my death. I should be appreciative of their remarks. I do love them, and they are an important part of my life. The sarcastic wit blended with their genuine admiration, kept me connected to a world beyond the stage. They will say, "I was assertive, poignant, with beautiful arms."

Yes, that was what the writer at the *Times* had to say in a recent article, "She has the loveliest arms in American ballet." He was likely a good representation of where modern audiences have shifted their focus. It is now the appearance of the dancer that defines the beauty of the ballet, and not so much the talent.

The family is busy preparing the house for the Festival of Lights. I feel the guilt from missing so many of the Hanukkah nights. The ballet company traveled during the wintertime, and we often missed the family settings. While they shared gifts and blessings and delighted at the taste of latkes and sufganiyot jelly donuts, I often sat alone sipping tea in the legendary Ritz Paris hotel.

Today I lay in my bed with my eyes closed, and the faces of a thousand students are asking "Where are you? When will you return?" How can this be my epitaph? My once taunt skin clothed in the silk leggings of brocaded tutus, held the attention of men and women alike. I am not meant to be a decrepit dying woman, I proclaim to myself. I am the personification of beauty and the purveyor of the human spirit. Yes, I want to scream, but I just lie here listening to the rasping sounds of my breath that underscore the reality of my impending death.

I am exhausted by the flow of daily visitors and their well-meaning but repetitive mantra, wishing me strength and faith. I should be more thankful for their sympathy, but the time for positive uplifting encouragement has passed. If they were to speak honestly, they would simply be saying *Metloya Lak* "Goodbye Melisa, may you find peace."

It's December 15th, 2006, and the first night of Hanukkah. I will be here in my home for the lighting of the *shamash.* Only God knows if I shall survive until the illumination of the last candle. As they burn their length and melt away, my light on earth will fade as well. I am slowly giving up the physical battle with a sobering level of acceptance, but my heart has not opened up to the spiritual embrace of death. I am too tired to weep, and my mind will not yet accept an eternal heavenly slumber.

My last visitor is a big surprise. I asked my husband to help me slowly sit up in bed, and my eyes hungrily took in the delightful reassuring smile of the iconic Rabbi Rubenstein. Why he would be here with me was beyond my understanding. My husband must have had something over on him. I was deeply moved by his visit, but it also brought a sense of finality to my thoughts of death.

Still, here he was at my bedside, holding my hand and reciting Psalm 121. "Shir la-ma-alos, eso aynai el . . . A song for ascents. I shall raise my eyes to the mountains, from where my help will come. My help is from the Lord, the maker of heaven and earth."

My husband Don rose from his chair, just as the lights went out. He stumbled forward into bed.

I held him and asked, "What happened? Are you okay?"

He replied, "The power went out. Maybe it will only be a brief outage." The symbolism that came with the power failure was not lost on me.

I felt a chill and was suddenly overcome with emotion and said, "Please don't get up. Hold me. Please just hold me."

Rabbi Rubenstein put his hand on Don's back and continued his prayer, "The Lord is your guardian; the Lord is your protective shade." I felt at ease. My husband was trembling, and the prayer continued. "The sun will not harm you by day, nor the moon by night." My heart was racing, and each breath was an exaggerated gasping intake of air.

The lights were still out, and I could see the candelabrum and its single flickering flame. I held my shivering husband tight and thought again that I would not make the final lighting of the *shamash.* Just as the candles slowly melted, I knew my life's spirit was also slipping away. In my mind's eye, I could see everyone in my life: my parents, the children, and the dancers. They were all here. I could feel their presence and hear their voices as they paraded across the stage in my mind. They waved and blew the kisses of a final goodbye. I felt a moment of mindful peace sweep over me, as though a great weight had been lifted from my body.

The power was abruptly restored and light filled the room. As my eyes adjust to the flickering brightness, I realize that I'm not dead. I feel the rabbi's hand and my husband's warmth. I don't speak aloud, and for a moment I want to return to the place of solitude, but the question looms, "What now? Will I know an eternal life in heaven?"

Rabbi Rubenstein stops the prayer and, looking into my eyes, he says, "Your time on this earth is sacred. Your thoughts and deeds have helped and inspired many souls. Your light will shine for generations to come." I clasp my hands around his and look up at him. He can see the shimmering tears in my eyes. He continues. "You will have life eternal. You will be gathered with your people, and before the afterlife of Olam Ha-Ba, you will return and continue your light. When the demons are banished, the Messiah will come for you, and you will enter the heavenly realm of Gan Eden for your eternal life in heaven."

Rabbi Rubenstein stands back from the bed and holds his hands together in silent prayer. So, there it is. Eternal life is mine. I can die, but I do not die. Cancer cannot kill my soul. I may now leave this world in peace. While I struggled to accept that my time on earth is over, I am now more settled with the comforting revelation of eternal life.

I reach for my husband and pull him close. My eyes are flooded with mixed tears of love and sorrow. "My dear husband, I will leave you soon but set aside your pain and know that I have always loved you. We will come together again and be with our people. We will hold each other in the Heavenly Garden as our ultimate reward. I pull him tightly to my chest as though he is my final connection to this world. I whisper sweetly in his ear, "It is now time to let go. "Know that I am yours forever. *Hanukah sameach my love*"

Written for the family of Melisa Hayden (1923-2006)

The Christmas Light

As I pulled my car into the driveway of my parents' home, my head began a painful drumroll. The pounding was intense and, as suddenly as it came, the pain and pressure stopped. I had been stressed over the days leading up to the family gathering. I had guessed that the headaches were the result of the anxiety and told myself, "You can do this. It's only two days. Just smile and nod and stay calm."

Christmas Eve was a gloomy sort of day, and keeping the holiday spirit alive was difficult. It was not supposed to be this way. I should be with my wife, my son, and my daughter. The weeks before Christmas were filled with upsetting events that came with the legal aspects of our separation and divorce. Overwhelming feelings of guilt had robbed me of sleep and raised my daily stress level.

My parents were devastated when my wife left and took the children to her family home in Birmingham. I deserved the outcome; I had put her in an impossible situation and her dignity and sense of self-worth were on the line. I knew the move was just as painful for her and the children as it was for me. My own feelings of guilt were now crushing any inkling of holiday spirit in my life.

My brother and sisters and their spouses traveled to our parent's home for the annual family Christmas celebration. The closeness of our relationships has grown more distant over the last couple of years. The sleeping arrangements for the holiday would effectively close any sense of physical distance. My brother stayed at a friend's house nearby, and my two sisters, their husbands, and I, squeezed into the guest bedrooms at our parent's house. When we were younger, without as much troubling history, the arrangement offered a wonderful chance to reconnect with each other, and to share new stories and past memories.

In the past, family dinners were lively and played out like a televised comedy show. This year, things were very different. We were generally unhappy people. The dinnertime laughter and humorous exchanges of exaggerated criticism have been replaced with periods of uncomfortable silence and muted sideline conversations. Dad spoke on and on about the latest world news, but he rarely asked questions or spoke directly to any of us. That was his way of avoiding the trauma and conflict that hovered in a cloud above the dining table.

Each of us had some sort of family grievance, but mine was overarching the classic issues experienced by most families. When my wife moved out and took our children with her, my parents lost their grandchildren and I lost my sense of wellbeing and hope for a happy future. The glumness of the holiday was overwhelming and I wanted it to be over so I could go back home. *Home?* I asked myself. *What was I thinking, my home no longer exists*. I could feel the pain in my head returning.

Dinner was a family affair, and as usual, my mother did most of the cooking. All the old Christmas songs played on an antique phonograph in the living room, but even Sinatra and Bing did little to lighten the mood that evening. My brother tried to amuse us with his playful antics and off-color jokes, but the most he could evoke from me was a muffled chuckle.

After dinner, my younger sister and I pitched in to help clear the table and wash dishes. Dad came in and began talking about how different things were without my wife and kids there. I knew where that conversation would lead and tried unsuccessfully to engage him in other topics. My sister diffused the tension by dropping a porcelain dinner plate that shattered on the tile floor. I am reasonably certain that she did this intentionally—she was strangely helpful in that way.

As everyone began preparing to retire, I filled a water glass half full of Remy Martin and slipped quietly upstairs to my assigned room. As I sat there on the edge of the bed, I thought through the last two years and everything I should have done differently. My work kept me away from home during most weeks. On the weekends I would retreat to the den and television with a regular dose of my favorite scotch whiskey on ice. The combination of my work schedule and bad behavior also put my marriage "on the rocks."

Over the past year, my relationship with my dad and mom had also deteriorated to an uncomfortable level. They were clearly disappointed in me, and Dad had no reservations about telling me what my shortcomings were. He would start most sentences with "You should have . . ." or "It's too bad you didn't handle this differently . . ." I was hurt by the failure of my marriage; I painfully missed my wife and children. I was even more surprised at how quickly the close and supportive relationship that I had with my parents so abruptly diminished.

The Cognac dulled my senses enough to fall asleep. After an hour of sleeping partially clothed, on my back with my mouth slightly open, I was abruptly awakened by a sharp pain in the base of my neck. It was more intense than anything I had ever experienced. I lay there thinking that I might be having a heart attack. I held my wrist in one hand and checked my pulse. It was pounding away, too rapid and erratic to count. I moaned and tried to call out, but could only manage make a monotone buzzing sound. I was no longer thinking about the Christmas dinner or the miserable situation I had created for my family. The pain was something new and unlike any physical ailment that I was familiar with. My legs were quivering, and I felt paralyzed and could not move from the bed.

I struggled onto my side and crashed to the floor, as I rolled off the bed. I found the cord charging my phone and pulled it from the nightstand onto the floor. My hands felt numb as I fumbled with the phone. I punched in the numbers 911 three times before getting it right. I wasn't panicking, but the pain was so intense I felt as though my head would explode. The 911 operator could hear the raspy garbled sounds coming from my mouth.

I tried desperately to utter the words, "Stroke, I'm having a stroke!" She understood enough to know it was a medical emergency. She responded, "Help is on the way. Please stay on the line with me. Is there anyone there with you?"

I made more unintelligible sounds. Yes, there were people here, but they could not hear me. I tried to bang my foot against the floor but my legs were shaking so badly, the sound was muffled and not heard by anyone in the room next to mine.

The paramedics arrived quickly and banged on the front door. They shouted, "Are you there? Can you hear me?" The banging sound and the loud voices on the ambulance's radio awakened everyone. My oldest sister, Susan, was the first downstairs and she unlocked the door. She had no idea why they were here. I could hear them talking but I could not speak. I dragged myself to the bedroom door and partially into the hallway near the top of the stairs. I pushed the door hard against the wall, but the doorstop muted any noticeable sound. With great effort, I managed to make an odd-sounding noise from deep in my throat. It sounded like a wounded animal. Luckily it was enough to get the attention of the EMT, who immediately bolted up the stairs. She took my hand and checked for a pulse, then lifted my eyelids to observe my pupils. She prompted me through preliminary field tests for a stroke. The EMT spoke into her collar microphone and turned back to me with reassuring eyes.

She said, "I got you. Try to be calm."

She placed her arm under my head while the other paramedic shifted my body onto a portable stretcher. The two EMTs struggled to move me down the stairs. My sister held the door, and they carried me to a waiting ambulance in the driveway. My parents were sequestered in a remote wing of the house and came to the doorway just as the ambulance was pulling away.

An injection administered by the paramedic worked quickly to stabilize my enormously high blood pressure. My legs stopped shaking and I was conscious but could only lay there in a motionless dream like state. I do not remember the ride to the hospital or being moved from the ambulance to the emergency room. There were several people around my bed, and they were frantically setting up an IV and placing cardiac monitoring pads on my chest and abdomen. I was there but I had no role. My mind was blank. I had no anguishing thoughts or great fear. To have a thought at all was a challenge.

Later that night, I was awake and looking around my bed, I could see the IV tubes and wires attached to my body. My shaved chest had a dozen uncomfortable pads with wires that slipped through the armhole of my undersized hospital gown. The drugs that were administered in the ambulance and ER had reduced my blood pressure and relieved the crushing pain at the base of my neck. Now I was awake, alive, scared, and alone. I remembered being at the top of the stairs and hearing the comforting sound of the EMT's voice.

"I got you. Try to be calm." Her words somehow bridged a gap between me slipping away to darkness, and the world of the living.

The room was not completely dark; a dim light allowed me to see through the glass doors and out to the nurses' station. The machines periodically made clicking sounds and humming noises while monitoring the IV drip lines and my blood pressure cuff. The heart monitor sounded an alarm whenever I coughed or tried to roll onto my side. The loudest noise came from the pumps that inflated the plastic wraps on my lower legs. Had it not been for the administration of drugs, remaining calm in this surreal setting would not have been possible.

I was trying to clear my head and think, *What happened to me? Where is everyone?* I could see the nurse's station, and they were busy talking and looking at their computer monitors. Their workstation was surrounded with more monitors and siren like lights on the ceiling. I was beginning to gain a level of awareness and clarity of thought. I was becoming anxious but not because of my condition. I was thinking about my wife and children. *Where were they? Were they okay?* My mind was still confused, and I was becoming afraid for the first time since the incident. Not so much afraid for what my own outcome might be, but terrified about what I might be leaving for my wife and children.

It was Christmas Eve, and the hospital staff was not in full force. Most physicians were home with their families. Those on call were busy with the usual holiday emergency room accident victims. Except for the medical monitoring hardware sounds, the cardiac intensive care unit was fairly quiet. A janitor passed slowly by the glass wall of my CCU room, quietly buffing the hospital corridors. Everything seemed almost normal. Well, I thought to myself, there was nothing normal about this. I have no idea how much time has passed since the ambulance ride. I wondered if it had it been hours or an entire day.

Where is my family? I don't want to be alone.

I heard a thud, like a muted explosion, and the light that had dimly illuminated the room was now dark. The machines stopped humming and flashed tiny amber lights on and off. We had lost electrical power. I heard what sounded like engines coughing and starting and then dying. I could hear people in the hall shouting and rummaging around, opening and slamming drawers. The overhead emergency lights were illuminated at the hallway ends, but the light did not reach the center section of the large building.

In the darkness, I could hear the footfalls of people running in the hallway outside my room. With the air no longer moving, I could smell the strong antiseptic fluid that was used to clean the room's surfaces. Fortunately, air continued to flow into the nasal pillows that supplied oxygen to my lungs. Someone opened the curtain to my room and pointed a flashlight in my direction but left as quickly as they'd appeared.

I tried to remain calm and thought things would all settle down, the lights would come on, and doctors and nurses would be back in to check on me. Minutes passed and no one came. The pain in my neck slowly started to return and my anxiety rose with each breath. I searched in the darkness for the nurse call button. It was on the floor beyond my reach. I sat up in bed and wanted to stand, but my legs began to quiver and then shake more violently. I fell back on the bed and felt frozen and unable to move. I instantly had the feeling that I was dying. I thought, *This is what it's like. This is how I will die—all alone.*

I stared into the darkness above my bed. In my mind I could see my wife, and I wanted to reach up and touch her. I wanted to tell her how sorry I was for making such a mess of our lives.

Two people rushed into the room. I could hear them talking but could not make out the words. Portable lights gave them an eerie glow. I felt them pulling and probing my body. I suddenly felt very cold. Then I felt nothing.

A nurse spoke loudly saying, "I'm not getting a pulse. Code Blue! Code Blue!"

Now I was weightlessly floating above the bed and watching the frantic people below. I looked down thinking, *I don't want to die.* Time stood still. I could hear a hundred jumbled voices. The images of everyone I had ever known in my life flashed through my mind. I could not speak. I was floating on a cloud, standing upright, and a bright but very pleasant light held my attention. I calmly thought, *I must be dead.* I will never see my family again.

A soft friendly male voice called my name, and calmly said in a poetic tone, "Don't be afraid. You are safe now."

Then there was a peaceful silence. After what seemed like many minutes, the voice said more sternly, "It's not your time. You must go back."

I was instantly back in the hospital room, hovering above the bed. I looked down at the doctor and nurses and then just as quickly, my head was on the pillow. I opened my eyes, and my parents were there. My mother held my hand tightly in both of hers. She was praying that I would live. My father was standing next to her. He put his hand on my shoulder. This physical connection was more than a warm loving touch. I felt as though it was a forgiving and healing connection to a new life for me and my family.

My mother offered a tense smile and said, "We lost you."

She could barely speak.

My father leaned toward the bed and said, "Welcome back son. We love you."

The sound of his voice gave me the sense that this was indeed a new beginning for all of us. I slowly lifted my mother's wrist and lightly kissed the moist skin on back of her hand.

I spoke slowly, shakily saying, "Merry Christmas, Mom. I love you too."

Father's Day

When young men become fathers, there are no Dad Certification classes. Except for the reluctant participation in a Lamaze breathing session or two, the new dad is on foreign ground. For the lucky ones that had a dad in their home when they were growing up, becoming a father provides a deep and broadened perspective of the kind of man your father really was. You quickly come to understand the sacrifices that he made over the years and the difficulty that comes with making tough-love decisions for a child. As children, what we did not know at the time was that our dad—guided by a love for his children—was also growing and learning as we grew up together.

I was blessed to have both my parents lovingly guiding my development in the formative years. I am even more blessed that they are still with me. If I was ever a problem for my mom, all she had to utter was the phrase, "Wait till your dad gets home!" That was the end of whatever unacceptable behavior I was exhibiting. It wasn't as though he commanded respect, it came naturally. He was the provider and the keeper of knowledge. He was the foundation upon which we built our own confidence and desire to be a good child in his eyes, to grow up to be the right kind of man or woman. The virtues of honesty, respect, and hard work were instilled by his living examples in life.

My dad taught me hundreds of life lessons—he still does. He taught me to think analytically, but with the understanding that you must take action and make decisions at some point. For example, if I was at a point of indecision, he would say "Don't just stand there, *do* something, even if it's wrong." He knew from his own experiences that making mistakes was a productive part of the learning process.

Dad was my catcher when I pitched. He taught me to shoot, hunt, and fish. I learned about boats, rivers, and oceans. I had the freedom to explore the world on my own, knowing he was right behind me all the way. If I was wrong, he would correct me. If I needed help, he was always there. If I was lost, he would find me.

My father showed me the difference between right and wrong, not with a lecture or a list, but by the example of his own life. His ability to distill the complexities of most subjects and situations to simple, comprehensible corollaries that I could understand was a blessing. There was a level of tolerance in his teaching. He would say things like, "You can do it that way, but you will have to do it over after it fails." Or, "You do what you want, but I would do it the other way." There were countless examples of me proving him to be right in these assertions.

I was a successful, but unlikely, leader in the business world. With a mildly introverted personality, I often lacked complete confidence in my ability. Dad was my guide. He cleared many paths in his career that I walked down with confidence. At the height of my career, while receiving a "Business Hall of Fame" award, I told the audience of business leaders, "It's not hard to be a great farmer if the field has already been plowed." My dad was in the audience that day, and I hoped that my remarks gave him a sense of pride in his accomplishments, and hopefully mine as well.

My dad will be 93 this fall. He and Mom have been together for 75 years. Their children, grandchildren, and great-grandchildren, represent what family values should look like. The values he and my mother passed down to my generation are now passed on to the new generations of the Autrey family. My childhood was a chapter in their American Dream.

My life is not a replica of my dad's success and could never be. I am happy I had the opportunity to be a part of their life.
Dad, it is your day! Savor it, and know I love and admire you, and all that you and mom have accomplished.

Your son,
Ron Autrey
December 18, 2025

The Plight of the Hummingbird

My wings are tired and sore, but I refuse to feed from the human troughs with the throngs of young irreverent birds. The long trips to the forest in search of wild nectar producing flowers has worn me down and I fear that I am near the end of my days. Once upon a time, I was a young, vibrant hummingbird. My abilities to dart, jump, and soar at supersonic speeds were unparalleled in the bird kingdom. Like most of my fellow hummingbirds, I was beautifully feathered with divine artistry and painted in God-given colors. The world was our flower, and we basked in the beautiful forests and natural gardens. Life as a hummingbird was wonderful. We never anticipated that well intentioned gifts from man would bring more despair than bounty. As grand pollinators, we flew daily, from garden to garden, flower to flower. We spread life and beauty and distributed life-sustaining pollen to thousands of floral settings.

As the human population developed and expanded, they removed forests and built homes. They planted gardens and grew new flowers. Upon discovering our secret talents and beauty, they placed brightly colored replicas of flowering plants that hung from the trees and roof decks. We soon found that the intricate plastic flower replicas, while not real, still contained wonderfully sweet nectars.

Young birds swarmed the plastic bounty with abandon. Their flapping wings collided as they crowded around the plastic feeders. The manufactured nectar dripped from their greedy beaks. I cautioned them and told them they must not give up on our time proven mission of pollination. The world and all its beautiful plants and flowers depended on the steadfast execution of our role as grand pollinators. The young birds did not listen. Their days became shorter with less exploration and pollination as they siphoned the human gifts of free nectar.

When the nectar was consumed, the humans refilled the troughs. Day after day, the lives of the suburban dwelling hummingbirds became increasingly easier. They perched lazily on shaded porches and tree limbs and no longer needed to fly all day in search of flowers to feed their hunger. The children were born into the same leisurely lifestyle. The daily exertion of harvesting and pollination was now unnecessary. Life-giving nectars were provided freely and in abundance by the humans. The young pollinators became dependent on the human supply of life sustaining nectar. They did not suspect that the bounty from this new world could end at any time with cascading destruction of our bird families.

At my age, I realize that things can change quickly. The challenges of finding flowers in the dense forests were never easy, but it is what we were put on this earth to do. The days of happily flying about and seeing new worlds were slipping away. With free sustenance, travel was no longer required. Many of the older grand pollinators had also become spoiled by freedom from work. Our children no longer know about or understand how things used to be. They will never know the joy of finding the special flowers in secret gardens deep in the forest. The pleasant gatherings around luscious flowering bushes have been replaced with angry desperate birds fighting for a place in line on the suspended dishes of plastic flowers.

The wisdom of the elder birds is no longer passed down to new generations of pollinators. The happiness and satisfaction from the labor of a day of good flying and pollinating was gone forever. The feelings of guilt and inadequacy no longer motivated the older birds to promote or insist on exploration by the younger pollinators. With significant declines in daily pollination, the natural gardens in the forest were a dull grey and colorful nectar producing flowers became scarce. The young hummingbirds became increasingly bitter and angry and fought with each other over the plastic flowers and nectar provided by the humans. There was nothing the elderly pollinators could do. They could no longer explore new lands and provide for the growing numbers of incapable young birds. The decline in the quality of life in our society of hummingbirds was apparent and irreversible.

As time passed, many of the once beautiful houses and gardens built by humans were now older and crumbling. Some houses no longer filled the plastic reservoirs with lifesaving nectar. The empty feeders swung freely in the wind. The infighting over any available nectar became fierce. The larger, stronger hummingbirds often prevailed over the weaker starving birds. I recently witnessed a despicable scene where young birds were attacking the older pollinators as they tried to enter the porches where the plastic flowers and feeders were located. Even the younger birds were suffering and now dying at a younger age. Without pollination, the forests changed and the once flowering bushes were dry and barren. Weeks turned into months and years, and fewer and fewer flowers could be found. The animals that used to frequent the gardens were now also gone.

The young hummingbirds did not know how to hunt for new gardens, and the number of wild gardens continued to decrease.

Tall concrete towers of people replaced the houses that once provided the free life-giving nectar. Trees that surrounded us and provided shade from the blistering sun were now gone. The flora and fauna we once knew was rapidly fading toward extinction. The plight of the hummingbirds was now on a similar path of destruction.

The cohesive flocks of grand pollinators were in a state of decline. Our society of birds splintered into smaller disassociated groups of hummingbird families. Some of the more dedicated birds tried to teach the others how to hunt for flowers. Some clans of pollinators were phenomenally successful, while others faded away. Many of the self-sufficient pollinators left the dying forest and did not return to teach the younger birds how to survive. Birds who had nothing and lacked the skills to survive on their own lived among those who worked hard every day to provide for their clan. A much smaller third group of overprivileged hummingbirds were protected by humans who still had fine houses and flowering gardens.

Hummingbirds were now dying along with the dried up brittle grey plants that once produced the life-giving flowers. The sight of dead birds on the forest‘s floor is an image that will forever haunt me.

Looking back on the good years, I realize that the society of grand pollinators thrived on hard work, personal efforts, and the bounty of the natural forests and gardens. We happily fulfilled our role in the divine design of our avian universe. The introduction of food without work, as delightful as it seemed, was the downfall of our world. The destruction was caused in part by man's misguided benevolence, and in total finality by the collapse of our system of values.

Perhaps some of our kind will survive; and knowing the lessons we learned, perhaps they can start a new generation of grand pollinators that learn the value of work and living off the land. As easily as a generation of young birds was led astray, the next generation of grand pollinators may still learn their true purpose in life. The lesson for future pollinators must be that if humans can provide all we want; they can just as easily take away all that we need. I pray that the strongest of our leaders fly down from their perch and show the willing young birds how to not only survive, but to thrive in the natural beauty and bounty of the great forests.

Ron Autrey

www.ingramcontent.com/pod-product-compliance
Lightning Source LLC
Chambersburg PA
CBHW021623030826
48979CB00036B/1760/J

9798988188162